Make MINE

— Emma —
A cocky billionaire,
a sweet virgin, and lots
of spanking... sounds
hot to me!
♡ Elyse Kelly

ELYSE KELLY

Making Her Mine
Heated Novella Series Book 1
Copyright © 2021 by Elyse Kelly

All rights reserved.

The unauthorized reproduction, transmission, or distribution of any part of this copyrighted work is illegal. No part of this book may be reproduced in any form or by any means without the express written permission from the author, except for the use of brief quotations in a book review.

This literary work is fiction. Any resemblance to actual persons, living or dead, events, or establishments is entirely coincidental.

Cover Design: FuriousFotog
Editing: Pagan Proofreading
Formatting: Champagne Book Design

ISBN: 9798714517457 (print)

Making Her
MINE

CHAPTER 1

DREW

"Mr. Cohen, you have a call from Ms. Layla Malone? She says she's been trying to reach you on your cell." My administrative assistant's voice cuts in over my speaker phone while I sit at my desk.

Pressing the button on the keypad, I respond, "She has, and I blocked her number this morning. Please tell her to stop calling. You know how to handle these calls. Follow the normal protocol." Releasing the button, I relax back in my leather chair.

"Yes, sir. I'll let her know. I'll alert security as well. Anything else?" She's asking without asking if she needs to contact security at my penthouse, but the answer is no. It's always no because I never take them home with me.

"No, Carol, that'll be all. Thank you." Yes, I'm a cold bastard. But you don't get to where I am in this world without being this way.

Layla Malone is just one of many in a long line of one-night-stands. A beautiful socialite I slept with once, a few weeks ago. I'd seen her at several fundraisers and galas, and while I knew she was interested from the very beginning, I had kept my distance. She came on too strong for me and I could tell she might be a stage-five clinger.

I made sure to spell out the rules clearly and repeatedly right from the start, but obviously she heard what she wanted to hear. Hence the numerous calls to my cell afterwards and now the calls to my office. If she continues, I'll have her socially blacklisted. I don't have time to play games like that, but being a tech billionaire requires me to protect myself and my image.

Being the CEO of my own company didn't come without a fuck-ton of blood, sweat, and tears. I wasn't born into this world, but I damn sure fucking clawed my way in, and no one is going to take it away from me. So, yeah, I may be a fucking asshole, but I have to be to keep my place in this ever-evolving industry—which will eat you up, spit you out, and forget you ever fucking existed.

I'm not just a tech genius, but I'm also a cold, cunning shark in the boardroom—I'm not arrogant; these are just facts. I'm also known for being a growly bastard because I won't be led around by my dick or my heart. I take what I want, when I want it, and I will not accept any excuses. *This* is who I fucking am—take it or leave it.

Coming from nothing, I worked my ass off to have what I have. People see the money and the lifestyle and they think it was all given to me. *The fuck it was! I made this!* Men envy me and women want to be with me. They see my good looks and they think they can snag the unattainable, wealthy bachelor. But I don't do romance or relationships—just one night.

The rules are clear from the get go. There are no pretty lies that I'm going to call them because I won't. I won't be spending the night and they damn sure won't be coming over to my place. They get one night, and one night only—no repeats and no clingers. I've never had to blacklist anyone, but the threat alone is enough to make them go away. Just the thought that they won't get another invite to the "social event of the season" is enough to have them running away in their Louboutins.

My black cell phone vibrating on my desk pulls my attention away. Reaching over, I lift it up to see my best friend's name—who is also my CFO—on the screen. Pressing the green button, I answer the call. "What do you want, dickface?"

"Wow, to be a thirty-year-old billionaire, you still act like you're seventeen. And you must be alone because you called me *dickface*," Thomas says with humor in his voice.

"Aren't you observant?" I deadpan.

"You may be my best friend, but you're still an asshole."

"Then why are you calling me?" I ask. I look at the time on my computer screen and note that it's almost four o'clock on Monday afternoon. He's normally still in the office at this time, which makes me wonder why he's calling and didn't just walk in, especially since his office is around the corner from mine. Before I can ask, Thomas cuts in.

"I need a favor, man." He can't see me, but I raise my brow in suspicion. *This ought to be good.*

"Is that right? You don't ask me for favors often, so this must be good. What do you need?"

"My sister, Elissa, is coming to the city on Thursday and needs a place to stay for the weekend." He pauses and I wait him out. I've learned in business to just keep quiet and let the other party talk. Let them lay all their cards on the table first before you make a deal. "I don't want her to stay in a hotel in a strange city all by herself."

"I think you're being ridiculous. She's not a minor. I'm pretty sure she can stay in a hotel like a big girl," I tell him.

"I know she's not a kid, but she's my baby sister and I don't like the idea of her coming to the city alone and staying in some hotel all by herself. Yes, I'm being an over-protective bastard but I'm her big brother. I'd feel safer if she stayed with you."

"And why can't she just stay with you?"

"Because you sent me to San Francisco, dumbass. I'm overseeing the acquisition this week that *you* didn't want to do yourself." *Oh, yeah, I forgot about that.*

"Okay, but why can't she just stay at your place?"

"Because I'm doing some renovations while I'm gone." I hear Thomas blow out an exasperated sigh, clearly annoyed with me. "What's the big deal, man? You live in a fucking penthouse with plenty of space. Just show her around for a few days while she's there and I'll be there on Sunday to pick her up."

What he's asking really isn't a big deal to normal people, but I'm not a normal person. I like my space and I like my solitude. With the exception of Thomas, who's been my best friend since college, I don't really allow many people to get close to me. I find people are… disappointing and I prefer to do without them, rather than having to worry about them letting me down.

"Look, man, I know you aren't big on the whole family thing because your family is a bunch of assholes—which is saying a lot considering you're the biggest asshole I know—"

"I had to learn from someone," I joke with him.

"Keep telling yourself that. But seriously, my family is awesome. We've been friends for almost a decade and you've somehow managed to avoid meeting them. They're not monsters. And my sister is cool as shit. She's kinda shy and quiet—a book nerd really—but we're really close, even though she's five years younger.

"Do this for me, man. You owe me. Don't act like I haven't had your back all these damn years. Shit, I wouldn't even be out of town right now if it weren't for you."

"You're getting paid a shit-ton of money right now, so quit complaining," I remind him.

"I'm not complaining. I'm just saying that I'd be home this week when Elissa came to visit. But since I'm not, you're the next best thing. Now quit being a dick and help your best friend out."

"Fuck, fine already. If you'll quit whining about it, I'll do it. Just text me the details."

"Aww, you're the best friend ever. I—" I hang up on him. I may have a lot of money and I may be a grown ass man, but when it's just me and my best friend, we're still just two idiots.

I inhale a deep breath and blow the air through my mouth, closing my eyes as I try to relax. Leaning back in my black leather desk chair, I think about what I've just signed up for. The idea that I'm going to have some girl following me around like a puppy for a few days is enough to make my skin crawl.

I don't know anything about this girl. What if she's a slob? What if she has annoying habits like drumming her fingers on the table or picking her teeth? What if she talks too much? What the fuck have I gotten myself into?

CHAPTER 2

ELISSA

There was no reason for Thomas to book me a flight when I could've just rented a car and drove myself. The flight was only an hour, but it seemed silly when we only live about four hours away. But he said he didn't want me to spend the money on a rental and he'd rather not have me make such a long drive by myself. Sometimes, I think my big brother still believes I'm five years old with pigtails, asking to play with his Transformers.

Rolling my carry-on suitcase through the airport, I find where the rideshare drivers are located and pull up my app to request a ride. By the time I make it to the lane outside the airport, my driver is waiting for me. He loads my suitcase into the trunk and confirms my destination before we pull into traffic and head into the city.

This isn't my first time coming out here, but usually I'm with Thomas and staying with him. He's out of town on business and has arranged for me to stay with his best friend, who also happens to be his boss. I told him I could just stay in a hotel, but Thomas wouldn't hear of it. He hates the idea of me being in such a big city by myself. I don't know what the man is going to do if I move out here.

That's the whole point of my visit this time. I work for a publisher that has their corporate office here in the city. I do copy editing and proofreading for them, but I can do that from home. They'd like me to take on a bigger role doing developmental editing, but they want me to move here and work at the main office. I'm here to take a tour of the place, meet the team, and see if I'd like to move to the city.

I'm just going to be here for a few days, so staying in a hotel would have been just fine. After all, if I move here, I'll be living alone. Unless, of course, my brother has plans to try to get me to live with him. *Oh, shit! Does he think that? Oh, hell no!* If that is what Thomas Jones has planned, he has another thing coming. I guess we'll cross that bridge, if and when we get to it.

I really don't know much about Thomas's best friend, Drew. I've heard him talk about him over the years and of course curiosity made me look him up online. *Because who wouldn't Google a gorgeous thirty-year-old billionaire?* But I've never been the kind of person to give much credence to what you read online or on social media. So much of that stuff is made up or just a twisted version of the truth. All I know is that

I'm on the way to his penthouse and I feel way out of my league.

Drew Cohen is some kind of beautiful bastard genius with a billion-dollar tech company and I'm going to spend the next several days with him. I know he's a perpetual bachelor who doesn't date and is always seen with different women, but they're never too cozy in any of the pictures. The women always have a look of longing on their faces, and he always looks bored. *Talk about an ego-killer for a girl.*

I wonder what it would be like to be his girlfriend. All the girls I've seen him with are models or socialites. All tall and thin and beautiful. Definitely not like me. I'm on the taller side, but not model tall. And I'm what you call "thick" with lots of curves.

It's never bothered me though. I'm not big on dating—not because I don't want to, but because I've just never met anyone that made me feel like I wanted to spend my time putting in the effort. I guess that's why I'm a twenty-five-year-old virgin. But maybe if I move to the city, I'll finally meet a guy worth my time. Maybe a guy like my book boyfriends in the sexy romance novels I read.

"Miss? We're here," my driver says, pulling me from my thoughts.

"Oh, thank you." I unbuckle my seatbelt and exit the car. I meet the driver at the trunk, where he's removing my suitcase and setting it on the curb.

"Have a nice day, Miss."

"Thank you. You as well," I tell the driver, giving him a small wave. I grab the handle of my suitcase, pressing the button to allow me to extend the handle and roll my luggage behind me. I crane my neck up to take in the massive building before me. The architecture is beautiful with lots of glass.

I walk over to the main entrance and a doorman greets me, holding open the door for me. I know these are private residences, but I feel like I'm at some fancy hotel. The lobby is warm and inviting, but elegant with beautiful chandeliers and potted plants. There's a large desk directly ahead and a sharply dressed man waiting behind it.

"Good afternoon, Miss. May I help you?" he asks me. His voice is much kinder than I expected.

"Yes, I'm here to see Mr. Cohen. I'm visiting for a few days."

"Of course. Just a moment, please. Please help yourself to some refreshments while I give him a call." He gestures with his hand to a small buffet table off to the side of the lobby with fruit-infused water, coffee, and an assortment of small pastries and cookies. I'm not hungry, but I step to the side and give him some privacy to make the call—I assume to Drew—to confirm I am in fact supposed to be here. After a few moments, the man speaks, getting my attention.

"Miss Jones, we're happy to have you as Mr. Cohen's

guest." He slides a business card across the desk to me. "There is a private entrance on the side of the building and in the garage which our residents use. This code is for those doors as well as the private elevators. You'll need the additional code below that to take you to Mr. Cohen's penthouse. Mr. Williams here, will show you to the secure elevator that will take you to the penthouse.

"If you need anything during your stay, I am Mr. Black. I can be reached at any time, day or night, and my contact information is on the back of that card. Please don't hesitate to call me. It's a pleasure to meet you, Miss Jones." He offers his hand to me and I shake it in return. When I reach for my suitcase, Mr. Williams already has it and is waiting for me to follow him to the elevator.

We quickly cross the lobby and make our way to the bank of elevators. After I press the call button, it only takes a few minutes for the elevator car to arrive. Mr. Williams holds the door for me to enter the car, but doesn't get on with me. I take my suitcase and thank him before entering the code into the keypad to take me to the penthouse.

Looking at my reflection in the mirrored doors, I feel so out of my element. This is by far the fanciest place I've ever been. Then again, a billionaire does live here so what did I expect. Dressed in jeans, ankle boots, and a sweater, I feel way too casual to be meeting Drew for the first time. *Too late now, I guess.*

The elevator doors open and I realize they lead

directly into his apartment and not a front door. *No wonder there's a private code and Mr. Williams didn't come up with me.*

"Hello? Drew?" I call out to the silent penthouse. I suddenly hear footsteps approaching from my left and turn my head. I see him coming from down a hall and walking towards me. I can't see his face just yet, but God, he's tall—has to be at least 6'4"—and muscular.

He comes into the light and I can see him better. The moment his eyes lock onto mine, his steps falter a bit, but he quickly recovers and continues walking towards me. *My God, this man is beautiful!* I knew he was gorgeous, but pictures really don't do him justice. The figure approaching me is dressed in dark gray flat-front slacks, with a crisp white button-down shirt. He's not wearing a tie and his top two buttons are open with his sleeves rolled up, showing the most delicious arm porn I've ever seen.

Drew is tall with a lean, masculine, muscular build. His dark hair is trimmed into a perfectly styled undercut that's nicely faded on the sides and longer on top, combed back and slightly to the side. His face is cleanly shaved, showcasing that sharp, angular jawline that makes a girl crazy.

But it's those deep arctic-blue eyes that are so hypnotic I can't form a coherent thought right now. Suddenly I realize those eyes seem angry as they narrow their focus on me. I look down and see his hands clenching and unclenching at his sides.

"Umm, hi. I-I'm Elissa. Thomas's sister. Y-you must be Drew?" *Off to a great start, Liss.*

"Yes," he responds curtly.

"He told you I was coming, right? It's okay that I'm here?" I can see his nostrils flaring slightly as his breathing begins to subtly pick up. *Is he mad at me?*

"Yes."

"I... well, I... Look, I can see that this is gonna be a terrible inconvenience for you." I take a step back towards the elevator. "I'm just... I'm gonna go." I use my thumb to point over my shoulder, indicating my escape. This is a mistake and I don't know what Thomas was thinking. Panic starts to set in and beads of sweat start to form along my hairline. "I'll just get a hotel. I'm sorry to have bother—"

"Fuck no, you're not leaving. Your ass isn't going anywhere."

CHAPTER 3

DREW

I was in my penthouse office when Michael, my concierge, called. I meant to have Carol contact him with the details about Elissa's visit so she'd have what she needed waiting for her at the front desk, but I got tied up negotiating a new deal and it slipped my mind. If I'm honest, I think my subconscious made me forget because I've been dreading this shit.

Now I'm waiting for her to arrive. I know she's on the elevator because a security alert just went to my phone and my watch, as well as a chime sounded in the apartment, letting me know someone was on the way up. I should get up and go wait for her at the elevator like a damn gentleman, but I'm still being a pouty bastard.

"Hello? Drew?" *Fuck, her voice sounds sweet.* I push back my chair from my desk and stand to leave my office. Walking down the hallway, I see her standing just outside the elevator. I can't discern her features, but I take in her figure.

She's taller than average, maybe 5'7" or 5'8". The girl has curves for fucking days and an hourglass body that begs to be touched by my hands. Her thick thighs are encased in dark skinny jeans and she's wearing a white tank with a slouchy cream-colored, off-the-shoulder sweater, giving a hint of her smooth café au lait skin.

As I get closer, our gazes lock and I damn near trip over my own feet. Her honey brown eyes hold me in place and I feel like I can't move.

She's so fucking beautiful.

She's wearing her dark chocolate, wavy hair down, just past her shoulder blades. A few wispy pieces frame an angelic face with high cheek bones and full luscious lips. She may look like an angel, but her body's made for sin and I'm ready to dirty her the fuck up.

What the hell is wrong with me? One look at this girl and my brain is overloaded with thoughts of how I want to fuck her right here on my penthouse floor. Her skin looks like caramel and fuck, do I love caramel. I want to lick every inch of her and I just met her.

I need to calm the fuck down and get in control. I hate not being in control. *Get your shit together, Drew!*

"Umm, hi. I-I'm Elissa. Thomas's sister. Y-you must be Drew?"

"Yes." *Fuck, I think she's short-circuiting my brain.*

"He told you I was coming, right? It's okay that I'm here?"

"Yes." *Talk to her, idiot!*

"I… well, I… Look, I can see that this is gonna be a terrible inconvenience for you. I'm just… I'm gonna go. I'll just get a hotel. I'm sorry to have bother—" *She's gonna leave, dumbass!*

"Fuck no, you're not leaving. Your ass isn't going anywhere." I pinch the bridge of my nose and hang my head. I'm better than this. I've never been more attracted to a woman in my fucking life, but I am *not* this guy. Taking a deep breath, I try to calm my inner caveman thoughts which are warring with the ideas of all the ways I want to fuck this girl.

"I'm sorry, Elissa. I think we got off on the wrong foot. Why don't you come in?" I take her small suitcase from her and place my hand on her lower back, leading her into the sitting room. It doesn't escape my attention how good it feels to have my hand on her body or how warm she feels to my touch. "Have a seat and I'll take this to the guest room."

She nods and sits on the chaise, giving me a tentative smile before I head off down the hall. I have multiple rooms in this place, but the only room I want her in is mine. If I told her that though, it'd probably scare the shit out of her. I guess if she has to be in another room, I'll put her in the one next door—I won't allow her to be any farther away from me than that. And it's only going to be for one night. Because after that, she will be mine.

I've never in my life had this kind of reaction to someone before and I feel like I've been struck by lightning. But there is only one word that keeps repeating in my head right now and that word is "mine." I want to make her mine. I need to make her mine. But I know if I told her the thoughts in my head, she'd run out of here screaming.

I wouldn't blame her… I sound crazy. I'm sure I even sound like some of the women I've slept with. But I can't explain it—I have to have her. Something primal deep inside me needs her. Her soul calls to mine, and it's like as soon as I was in her presence, my soul recognized hers. I *will* have her. And soon.

Reluctantly, I leave her luggage in the room next to mine before walking back out to the sitting room. I find she's kicked off her ankle boots and tucked her legs underneath her on the chaise, while reading a tech magazine that has me on the cover. She looks so relaxed and perfect, like she belongs here in my home and I fucking love it.

"Don't believe the hype," I tell her, coming around and sitting down next to her.

"According to this, you're kind of amazing," she says, looking a little sheepish, maybe a bit embarrassed to be reading about me.

"You can just ask me anything you wanna know. I

won't hide anything from you. There will never be secrets between us, Elissa." My voice takes on a deep tone. I watch her body quiver ever so slightly and I'm pretty sure if her sweater weren't so thick, I'd see her nipples pebble beneath it.

"I… um, the things I'd wanna know… I doubt they'd be in here," she says, closing the magazine and setting it down on the table.

"Is that right?" I pause, looking my fill and letting my heated gaze roam her body. I know that I'm being an ungentlemanly bastard but I don't care. Might as well let her know now that I want her, so she can be prepared. I'll give her time to get used to the idea, but I won't give her long before making her mine.

"Why don't we have dinner here tonight and we can get to know each other better. How's that sound?"

"That'd be perfect. It was a short flight, but I did some work this morning before I left and I'm a bit too tired to go out."

"Okay. Go freshen up while I order something. Just meet me in the kitchen when you're ready." I stand and offer her my hand to help her up. She looks up at me with those beautiful eyes and I envision this is what she'll look like when she's sucking my thick cock. The fucker twitches in my slacks and I will it to calm down, especially since she's currently eye-level with it.

She takes my hand and stands gracefully. Unable to resist, I lift her knuckles and place a gentle kiss on the back of her fingers. "I'm sorry about how we first met. You surprised me, and I'm rarely surprised."

"Oh. A good surprise?" she asks shyly.

"Best surprise of my life, baby. Go on, get ready for dinner. I'll see you in a minute." I release her hand and watch her full, round ass as she walks away. *I can't wait to get my hands on that ass. I wonder what she likes.*

Pulling my cell phone from my pocket, I walk to the kitchen. My chef prepares meals for me, which can be reheated, and leaves them in the fridge but I want something else for Elissa tonight. I'll give Michael at the front desk a quick call and he'll take care of everything for me. I want to impress her, but what the hell would she like?

She's not like other women. I know that she and Thomas come from a good middle-class suburban family from upstate. They're salt-of-the-Earth people—not the pretentious assholes I'm surrounded by most of the time. I don't think she'd care for some four-course, five-star meal right now.

Maybe I should just call Thomas and ask him what she likes. No, then he'll want to know why I'm asking him and not her. Then he'll think I'm hitting on his sister—which I am—and I'm pretty sure he'll want to kick my ass. *Shit!* I've never really been in this kind of predicament before and I've never had to actually work to impress a woman.

The sound of giggles makes me turn my head and

I see Elissa standing off to the side, watching me. I narrow my eyes and growl at her, which only makes her roll her eyes at me in return. She's obviously more comfortable with me now and that makes me happy, but I also want to spank her ass for sassing me. *Would she liked to be spanked?*

"Can't decide what to order? How about Chinese? It's my favorite," she offers, putting me out of my misery. "You looked like you might be having trouble deciding."

"Chinese is fine. What would you like?"

"How about you order for me. I wanna see what you'd pick?" This little bit of control she gives me is heady. Just wait until I take full control of her body later.

I order the food—way more than either of us could ever eat—and she loves every dish I have her try. Sitting next to her at the breakfast bar, I watch her gracefully use her chopsticks to place each morsel of food on her tongue. It's the most sensual thing I've seen in a long time. The way she closes her pillowy lips around each bite makes me want to see those lips around the head of my dick.

I'm impossibly hard through the whole meal while we share food and she offers to feed me tastes from her plate. With every brush of her hand and touch of her skin, my dick jerks and weeps precum. I'm dying to claim her right here, right now, but I know she's not ready. Fuck, I just met her and I know it's too soon, but I have to make her mine.

She pushes her plate away and gets off her stool. "This was wonderful. Thanks for dinner. I'll clean up." She reaches across me, the soft scent of her floral perfume filling my nose, as she grabs my plate and takes our dishes to the sink. I think it's time to give her a taste of what's to come.

I rise and follow her to the sink, where she's standing and rinsing the plates and glasses in preparation for the dishwasher. Standing behind her, I pull her hair to the side and ghost my lips across the back of her neck. As I press my massive cock that's harder than steel between her ass cheeks, she sucks in a quiet gasp. I run the tip of my nose up and down the column of her slender neck, inhaling the scent of her perfume and her warm skin.

When I lick her skin and gently nibble her flesh, her body quivers beneath me. I press a sweet kiss to her neck and say, "Let me finish this up, Liss. I know you're tired. You should go to bed."

I've almost caged her in, but I give her just enough room to turn around and face me. When she does, I see heat and desire and maybe a bit of curiosity in her eyes. I lean in like I'm going to kiss her lips and her eyes begin to close, but I tilt my head, kissing her cheek goodnight instead.

I let my lips linger against her skin for a moment longer than necessary before pulling back and seeing disappointment and confusion on her face. *She's right where I want her. Soon, baby. Soon.* I give her a cocky smirk and a wink.

"Go to bed, Elissa. I'll see you in the morning." I step back so she can get around me.

"Goodnight," she says, her chin slightly lifted, refusing to let her pride be bruised. *Good girl.* I smack her ass as she walks past me and I hear her moan softly, making my dick twitch. *Don't worry, baby. I'll hear more of those moans very soon.*

CHAPTER 4

ELISSA

I didn't sleep at all last night, tossing and turning, going to bed so confused and disappointed. And so, so wet. My pussy ached so badly all night and it's all his fault. *Damn him for being so gorgeous!*

I could've sworn when I first got here, he didn't like me. He just seemed so mad that he barely spoke a word. But he warmed up pretty quickly and put me at ease. And thank God, because I really didn't want to leave.

When I first laid eyes on him, I wanted to rip his clothes off with my teeth and beg him to take my virginity. I can't explain how my body responded to him, but it was like boom, instant heat filled my veins. Like I was on fire from the inside out and the need to feel his bare skin touch mine was so intense it almost overwhelmed me.

I've been around guys before and I may have kissed a few here and there, been on a few dates, but nothing to write home about. It's not that I'm unattractive or anything, it's just that I haven't found anyone that made me feel like the characters in my books. Yeah, I know that's stupid—they're fictional romance books. But they have to be based on some kind of truth, right?

Well, I'm glad I waited because the moment I saw Drew Cohen, I knew what I had been waiting for all this time. I can't explain it and I don't want to—I just know it feels right being with him. But I also know he's a one-night-stand kind of guy. I'm not sure how to proceed or even if I should.

Something deep inside me tells me I belong to him, though. To just let go and give myself to him. That what I'm feeling is beyond attraction and I think he feels it too. When he approached me after dinner, I felt his body's response to mine—there was no mistaking how hard he was, pressed against my ass.

I could feel his long, thick cock right between my cheeks as he nuzzled my neck. I was so turned on; my nipples tightened painfully as wetness seeped from my pussy. I was getting so obscenely wet I was afraid he'd smell how aroused I was becoming.

I turned around and I could see the lust in his eyes. He wanted me and I wanted him too. I thought for sure this was going to be it. And just when I thought he was going to kiss me, he didn't. *Bastard!* He kissed my cheek instead and told me to go to bed. *Go to bed!*

But then he spanked me when I walked past him. *The man is so confusing!*

So, I showered and went to bed horny and angry, and disappointed and confused. *Why did he stop? Could he tell I was a virgin? Is this some kind of game?* My insecurities and throbbing lady bits kept me up all night. Now I'm dragging ass and I've got to go to the corporate office for a tour and to meet the editing team, where my boss, Matt, is waiting to meet me at nine o'clock.

I shower in the en suite bathroom, which is bigger than my bedroom back home. I brush and style my dark wavy hair and put on tinted moisturizer and a few coats of black mascara. I finish my minimalistic look with a matte red lip before slipping on a black, fitted, sleeveless dress, a jean jacket, and taupe ankle boots.

Walking into the kitchen, I find Drew waiting for me and I'm surprised to see him there. I thought he had to work today and expected to catch up with him this evening. Maybe he's planning to go in to the office later this morning.

"I wasn't sure what you'd like, so I have a little bit of everything here," he says, pouring me a cup of coffee.

"This is for me?" I ask, shocked. "You didn't have to do this. I'm sure you need to get to the office." I take the steaming mug from him, our fingers brushing during the exchange and causing goosebumps to rise on my arms.

"I decided to take the day off. I thought maybe I'd

go with you to Lakeview Publishing, if you don't mind." My mouth drops open in surprise and my hand freezes mid-pour as I'm adding creamer to my coffee.

Regaining my senses, I ask, "Why? Aren't you busy?"

"I'm familiar with the company and I know some of the people over there. And I want to spend more time with you. Is that alright?" he asks, taking a step towards me with a predatory look in his eyes. I'd say he wants me, but after our almost kiss last night, I'm not so sure.

"Um, sure. Of course. I'll just… text my boss and let him know." I shoot Matt a quick message and explain who I'm bringing along with me. And because everyone knows who Drew Cohen is, he doesn't have a problem with the impromptu visitor.

We pick over the smorgasbord of breakfast foods Drew has laid out for us. After filling up and drinking our coffees, his driver takes us over to the Lakeview Publishing building a few blocks away from Drew's penthouse. It's like any other skyscraper corporate office you'd expect, with multiple businesses in the same building. We take the elevator to the appropriate floor following the instructions Matt texted to me, and check in with the receptionist at the front desk.

I notice right away that she's a pretty blond, slim and petite, wearing a tight, scoop-neck, sleeveless dress that should probably be worn with some kind of sweater or jacket for an office setting—but it isn't. She's cordial with me, taking my name and giving me a visitor's badge. Her smile is fake and not really reaching her eyes.

But she really turns on the charm when she sees Drew, and I want to claw her damn eyes out. I've never been jealous a day in my life—never had a reason to be—but I'm two seconds away from climbing over this desk and pulling her blond hair out. I must be making some kind of a face because Drew places his hand on my lower back—so low it's almost on my ass—and leans into me and says, "Down, girl. I'm here with you." I look up at him and he winks at me.

I narrow my eyes at whatever her name is, as she hands Drew his temporary badge. I force a fake smile before turning to give her my back, just as I hear my name being called from somewhere off to my right. I turn to see my boss, Matt, coming towards us and I walk over to meet him.

"Hi, Matt! It's so good to see you again," I tell him. I've only seen him in person a handful of times, but we have virtual meetings twice a month. He's a handsome guy in his early thirties, with sandy blond hair and ocean blue eyes. He's tall, but not as tall as Drew, and it's obvious that he works out. *I wonder if the receptionist has her boobs on display for Matt—which is fine, just keep those boobs away from Drew.*

"Hey, Liss! So glad you could make it." He pulls me in for a hug instead of a handshake. I think I hear a low growl come from somewhere and if I had to bet money on it, I'd say it was from Drew. "And you must be Drew. I'm Matt Anderson."

Matt extends his hand to Drew for a handshake, but Drew looks like he'd rather punch him in the face. After a second too long, Drew finally accepts Matt's hand and they have this kind of awkward shake, where they do some weird man communication thing with their eyes.

After the strange dick-measuring contest I just witnessed, they drop hands and Matt says, "We were on a different floor the last time you came by and the office has grown a lot since then. Lemme take you on a tour, Liss, and then you can meet the team." He turns to Drew and says, "You're welcome to wait here or come back later if you like."

I see Drew's jaw clench and his gaze sharpen. If looks could kill, Matt would be dead right now. Wrapping his hand around my hip, he says, "I'll stay with *Liss*, if you don't mind. It'll help us compare notes when we're making our decision later on." Last I checked, it was my decision, but this growly alpha side of Drew is melting my panties right off.

We follow Matt around the office for a tour and I fall in love with the place. Don't get me wrong, working from home is amazing. I set my own schedule, I get to wear my jammies, and I can work from literally anywhere. But being around other like-minded bookish people today was so much fun. I could be my true, book nerd self and didn't have to be embarrassed. *And who knew so many people love book smut, just like me?*

After the tour, and with great resistance from Drew, Matt treats us to lunch at a small restaurant around the corner. Even though we don't enjoy the same types of books, it's obvious Matt and I share a great respect for literature, writers, and all things book related. Drew participates in the conversation, surprising me with how much he knows about the industry. But it's his possessive actions that almost have me melting into a puddle on the floor.

Drew is sitting so close to me, our thighs are touching at the table. As if that isn't enough, his hand is resting underneath my dress on my bare leg, his fingers lightly brushing back and forth across the delicate skin of my inner thigh. Throughout the meal, his hand keeps getting higher and higher until his pinkie is almost brushing against my pussy lips.

By the time we finish our food, I'm ready to jump up from the table. My pussy is aching so badly and in need of relief. We wrap up with Matt and I thank him for the tour and lunch, promising to give him an answer on the job by Sunday. I give him a hug goodbye, and he shakes Drew's hand before he leans in and whispers something to him, too low for me to hear. Drew smirks at him and releases his hand, then wraps his arm around my waist, guiding me down the street to where his driver is waiting for us.

Getting into the car and sliding over in the back seat, I ask, "What did he say to you?"

"He said if I pissed on your leg to mark my territory, it might be less obvious," Drew says with a devious grin.

"What does that mean?" I ask, buckling up.

"You'll see, baby." He lifts my hand and kisses the back of it. I'm glad I came for this visit because I really loved the Lakeview offices. But more importantly, I'm loving every second I get with Drew. I don't know what any of this means and honestly, I'm a bit confused. I want him so badly, and I think he feels the same, but I just don't have the experience to know for sure. I've only been here a day and already I want to stay. And I want nothing more than to be his.

CHAPTER 5

DREW

Fucking Matt Anderson.

As soon as I saw that little shit, I knew what his game was. He wanted what was mine. I saw how he was flirting with her the whole time. She was so oblivious to it, too. Elissa had no idea the man was practically drooling all over her.

Well, fuck that! He can't have her. No one takes what belongs to me, and Elissa belongs to me. Tonight, she's going to know it. I will be claiming her and she will be staying here. So, that means she will be working with Matt. I think I made it very clear who she belongs to, but in case that fucker has any doubts, I'll make sure he knows she's taken.

I have plans for my girl tonight. I've wanted her since the moment I laid eyes on her, but I've given her all the time I can spare. I gave her a day and already some fucker tried to move in on my woman. Well, tonight I make her mine.

I had Michael make arrangements for dinner for us at a restaurant uptown. It's one of my favorite places and the wait-list is usually a year long. But I have a standing reservation and a chef's table with a private booth in the back. I'm taking her out to show her off and spoil her a bit. Then I'm bringing her back here and fucking her over and over again, until there is no doubt in her mind who owns her body.

We walk into the penthouse, and just like I asked, there are two boxes on the round table just inside the main entrance—a small shoebox sitting on top of a larger garment box, tied together with ribbon. Escorting Elissa over to the table, I gesture to the gifts and tell her to open them.

"They're for me?" she asks, surprised.

"Yeah, baby. Here, let's sit down." I pick them up and carry them over to the sitting room for her. Patting the cushion next to me, I indicate where I want her to sit.

Taking a seat, she tucks a leg underneath her and turns her body to face me. I hand her the gifts, and she starts with the smaller of the two boxes, untying the ribbon and pulling off the lid. Her hand flies to her mouth as she gasps, looking inside the box.

"These are *gorgeous*," she cries, picking up one of the satin Badgley Mischka jeweled, peep-toe pumps and clutching it to her chest. "Look at this color! It's stunning!" she says, gazing down at the shoe in her hands.

"You like them, baby?" I ask, already knowing the answer.

"Of course! But what are they for?"

"Open the other box." She carefully puts the shoes back in the box and places it on the table. I hand her the larger one and she opens it, setting the lid aside, before unfolding the tissue paper to reveal her next gift.

"Drew! Oh my God! It's beautiful!" She gingerly runs her fingers across the satin fabric of the peacock blue halter cocktail dress I had specifically picked out just for her. The color of the dress and the jeweled detailing at the waist is a perfect match to her shoes. "I… I don't know what to say." She peers at me, elated but slightly confused.

"Tonight is very special. And I'm taking you to one of my favorite places."

"Okay, but how did you know my sizes? You were with me all day, so how did you get these here?"

"I have enough money to get just about anything I want, Liss."

"Of course, you do," she mutters, glancing down. I lift her chin with my finger, forcing her to look me in the eyes.

"But there is something more important I want, that no amount of money can get me." I hold her gaze, stroking her jaw with my thumb.

"What's that?" she asks, breathily.

"You, Elissa. I want you. And I *will* have you." She

bites down on her full bottom lip and her pulse begins to beat wildly at the base of her neck. "I've been waiting to claim this sweet body of yours since the moment we met yesterday. I know you felt it, too. Didn't you? Tell me."

I take the dress from her hands and lay it on the table with the shoes. Moving closer to her, until our thighs are touching, I slide my hand beneath her hair and grab the nape of her neck. "Tell me."

"Yes, I felt it too," she says, her eyes half-lidded in lust.

"Do you want me? Do you want me to fuck that needy little pussy of yours?" I'm being a dirty bastard right now, but I don't care.

"Yes."

"Yes, what?"

"Yes, I want you." She's almost panting now. *Good.*

"Then go get ready. Take your time. I need to do some work, so I'll be in my office. Why don't you have some wine and take a bath. Relax and enjoy yourself." I massage her neck with my thumb and fingers. When she lets out a little moan, my dick jerks in response. "Save those sounds for later, baby. We'll leave here at six-thirty."

I look down at her plump lips just as her tongue darts out to wet them. Needing just a small taste, I lean in and press my lips against hers. I only meant to give her a chaste kiss, but she reaches for me, clutching my shirt and pulling my body toward hers. It turns me on even more and I lick the seam of her mouth demanding entry.

She doesn't hesitate to let me in and her sweet taste is like heaven. I'm exploring the depths of her mouth, tangling my tongue with hers, when I feel her move her body to straddle my lap. Right then, I know I need to stop us, or we'll never get to dinner. With herculean strength, I tear my mouth away from hers and rest my forehead against her chest as she sits on top of me, my dick straining in my pants beneath her.

"Tonight, baby. I promise." I wrap my arms around her waist so she doesn't fall and I stand, taking her with me. She drops her legs and I wait for her feet to reach the floor, before I let go of her. "You will be mine tonight, Liss. You better make sure that's what you want because there's no going back after that."

I kiss her lips once more before smacking her sweet ass and sending her on her way. Even if she's not sure, I'll do whatever it takes to make sure she knows that no matter what, she's mine.

* * *

Elissa looks like a fucking wet dream tonight in her dress and new shoes. The girl is stunning no matter what she wears, but tonight she turned heads at every table when we walked into the restaurant. The peacock blue color of her dress complements her creamy caramel skin tone so beautifully and she wore her hair up, showing off the halter neckline of the dress and even more of her soft, smooth skin.

Her legs are already long enough, but the four-inch, fuck-me pumps I bought her make her legs look a mile long. I want to bury myself deep inside her pussy while she wears nothing but those pumps as they dig into my ass and I pound into her over and over again.

Thank God, my private booth is at the back of the restaurant. We can see almost the entire dining room from our table, and unless you're looking for it, you won't really see ours. Once we were seated, I noticed she tried to put some space between us, but I squashed that pretty fucking quick.

She needs to know she belongs to me, and she's mine to do whatever the fuck I want with, even in public. I'll make her crave my touch. Make it so good for her that she'll want it all the time, even when people are around and can see. Soon, she won't be able to live without it and she won't give a damn where we are.

"Don't think you can get away from me, baby. You belong right next to me," I tell her, running my hand up and down her smooth thigh. Her skin is soft like silk and warm to my touch. I lean down and kiss her bare shoulder, watching as goosebumps appear on her arms. "So responsive. I fucking love it."

"You do?" she asks, looking up at me with her honey brown doe eyes.

Whispering in her ear, I tell her, "Take off your panties for me, Liss." I hear a small intake of air before she shakes her head no. "Take. Them. Off. Or there will be punishment later." I lean back, looking for her response.

I'm pushing her, not sure how she'll react to this. If we're going to be together—and we fucking are—I need her to get used to the way I am. I need her to know that I may be a dirty bastard, but I only want to pleasure her, even with punishments, and I'll never hurt her.

I massage her thigh and nuzzle her neck before gently pulling the lobe of her ear between my teeth. I lick the shell of her ear, then whisper, "I only want to make you feel good, baby. Even my punishments will get you off. I will never hurt you, Liss." I feel her body relax more with every word. "Now, be a good girl and take your panties off for me." This time she nods her head yes.

I slide away from her to give her some room and watch as her eyes dart around to see if anyone is watching. When she's satisfied that the coast is clear, she covertly slips her hands up her dress, hooking her thumbs into the waistband of her panties and pulling them from underneath her ass and over her thighs. Shimmying them the rest of the way down her legs, she discreetly catches them off her foot and balls them up in her fist.

I hold out my open hand to her, my palm face up in a gesture that clearly shows I want her to give me her panties. She hands over the tiniest black G-string I've ever seen and I wonder why she even bothered wearing the damn thing. When I cock my eyebrow at her, looking back and forth between her and her almost non-existent panties several times, she just giggles, knowing what I'm thinking. I shake my head and shove her panties into my pocket.

"I'm not sure if I should reward you for giving me your panties, or punish you because you almost didn't."

"Maybe… we could try both?" she says hesitantly, looking up at me through her thick black lashes. I pull her body over to mine.

"Is that what you want, baby?" She nods. "I want the words, Liss."

"Yes," she says, lust evident in her voice.

By this time our server comes over, bringing our meals to the table. We eat several courses and enjoy different wines with each course, careful not to overconsume. We both want to be clear-headed for what's to come later in the evening.

"Would you care for dessert or espresso this evening? Perhaps an apéritif?" our server asks.

"I couldn't eat one more bite," Elissa says with a satisfied smile on her beautiful face.

"I think we're all set," I tell him.

"Of course, Mr. Cohen. This will be added to your

tab. It was a pleasure to serve you both. Have a lovely evening."

"You as well." He excuses himself and leaves us. I never pay at the table when I dine here. Instead, I receive a monthly invoice because I come so frequently. Our service was excellent, as always, so I discreetly place two crisp hundred-dollar bills on the table underneath my wine glass for him.

"Shall we go?" she asks.

"You haven't had dessert yet," I tell her, a mischievous grin on my face. She cocks her head with a confused look. *This is gonna be so much fun.*

CHAPTER 6

ELISSA

Even though we've finished with our meal, we're still sitting at the table. Drew has this predatory look on his face like he wants to devour me, which he might, considering my panties have been in his pocket for almost the entire night. And my pussy is so wet it's dripping down my thighs and I pray it's not soaking through my new satin cocktail dress.

The chemistry between us is so explosive and we both know it's coming to a head. It's crazy and insane and happening so fast, but neither of us can deny it, nor do we want to. He says he wants to claim me and make me his, but the truth is I was his the moment he captured me in his deep arctic blue gaze. There's no sense in fighting it—I belong to him.

"You haven't had dessert yet," he says. He wraps his hand on the outside of my hip and pulls my body across the booth until I'm flush against him. He whispers in my ear, "When we get home, I'm finally going to fuck you, Elissa. It won't be soft and sweet like you probably need me to be, so I'll give you that now. Because when we get home, it's gonna be hard and fast and fucking dirty. Is that what you want?" His warm breath against my ear coupled with his dirty words and masculine hand massaging my inner thigh, all make a heady combination, causing my aching pussy to clench in response.

"You want that, don't you, baby? I can tell." His hand moves higher up my leg, two of his fingers lightly brushing the lips of my bare pussy. He pulls back and looks me in the eye. "Shaved or waxed?"

"Waxed," I pant. Swallowing loudly, I ask, "Is that what you like?"

"What do you like?" He uses all of his fingers to rub up and down my lips now and I can barely think straight.

"I p-prefer to wax. I-I like how it feels."

"You like how it feels when you touch yourself?" He rubs harder and I begin to roll my hips, seeking more friction.

"Yes," I hiss.

"That's fucking hot, Liss. I wanna see you touch yourself. Fucking yourself with your fingers until you get yourself off. Will you do that for me, baby?"

"Drew," I half whine, half beg.

"What, baby? What is it?"

"I… I need…"

"You need to come?"

"Yes." My voice is barely above a whisper. My hips are rolling more, but I'm trying to control it, seeing as how we're still sitting at a table in a public restaurant. I'm two seconds away from shattering apart and he's sitting here next to me cool as a cucumber, looking like just another romantic gentleman, whispering sweet nothings into his girlfriend's ear.

"Remember what I told you about punishments?" *Uh, what now?*

"Y-you said I'd enjoy them."

"Yes, this is the pleasure part of it. But it's still a punishment, Liss." He pulls his hand away from my pussy and I gasp, instantly missing his touch. My lips are aching, my clit is throbbing, and my nipples are so hard from arousal they could cut diamonds. He enjoys my misery by lifting his glistening fingers to his mouth and licking the digits clean. I can't help the frown that mars my face as I scoot away from him across the booth.

Smirking, he makes a tsking sound with his tongue and pulls me back to where I was sitting. "Do that again and I'll spank your ass later." The thought of his heavy, strong hand swatting against the bare skin of my firm ass has me squeezing my legs together, seeking relief. "Ooh, my baby likes that, don't you? Do you need to be spanked, Liss?" I don't answer. "I'll take that as a yes. Let's go."

He gets out of the booth first, then extends his

hand to help me up. Always the gentlemen, he offers me his bent arm as he escorts me through the restaurant, giving me plenty of time to keep up in my four-inch heels. His driver is waiting for us outside and holds the car door open as we climb in the back seat.

I know once we get back to the penthouse, everything will change. I'm ready for it, dying for it, and nothing will stop that. I've already made up my mind that I'm not leaving on Sunday. I'm taking the job and if Drew wants me as bad as he says he does, I'll stay with him forever.

* * *

Somehow, we manage to keep it together all the way back to the penthouse. But as soon as we step off the elevator, all bets are off. Before the doors even close, Drew presses my back against the nearest wall and slams his mouth to mine. This is no romantic kiss—this is a mouth-fucking kiss designed solely to show me whom I belong to.

He captures my face in his hands as his body cages me in, his hips grinding against me. I feel his thick, hard length rubbing against my lower belly, my soft breasts pressed to his muscular pecs. I want to feel his hot skin against mine and I'm frustrated that we're separated by clothes right now.

He reaches his hand underneath my dress, cupping

my sex hard. I drop my head back and moan with pleasure while he kisses along my jaw and neck and grinds the heel of his hand against my clit. Spearing my fingers through his dark hair, I pull his mouth back to mine, wanting more of his kisses.

He changes his grip on my pussy and begins sliding his fingertips up and down my soaking wet slit. *Fuck, it feels so good!* I've never been touched like this before and it's almost sensory overload. He circles my clit with his thumb and pumps two fingers in and out of my core.

"I can tell you're close, baby. Your greedy little pussy keeps sucking my fingers back inside and I can feel the pulse of your clit. Will you come for me?"

"Yes, yes," I pant, shamelessly grinding my pussy against his hand.

"Now, Liss. Come, now." Squeezing my inner walls, I come on his command. My core flutters for what feels like forever, especially since he denied me earlier at the restaurant. As I come back down, a fresh wave of wetness releases down my thigh and his hand. He gently slides his fingers out and shows me how they're coated with my cream.

He licks some of it off, humming his enjoyment. Then he holds his fingers up to my lips and says, "Open." I do as he commands and he places his cream-coated fingers in my mouth. "Suck." Feeling some strange kind of power, knowing that I can control his pleasure, I close my mouth over his fingers and suck them clean.

Never have I tasted myself before and the sweet, musky flavor, along with sharing this experience with Drew, is so damn hot. This man has awakened something deep inside me I had no idea even existed and I want to explore it with him. I have a feeling he's going to do so much more than just take my virginity.

"You taste so good, don't you, baby?" I nod. "Let's try something else."

He grabs my hand and tugs me towards the oversized chaise in the sitting room. Pulling me down to sit next to him, he immediately captures my mouth in another kiss. Just when I start to feel woozy, he breaks away and asks, "Do you trust me?"

"Of course. I know you won't hurt me."

"Good. Come here." He moves so he's sitting on the edge of the cushion and he positions me so I'm lying across his lap. When he said he'd spank me earlier, I thought he was kidding, but I guess not. I must admit, I'm excited and nervous, but I'm not afraid. I know he only wants to make me feel good and that he doesn't want to hurt me.

"I saw how you responded when I said I was gonna spank your ass earlier. You can say you don't want it, but you're a dirty girl and you like having your ass spanked, don't you?" I don't give him an answer.

"Hmmm. Quiet, I see," he says, running his hands up and down my ass and my legs, my dress pulled up with my bare cheeks on display. He begins kneading my fleshy globes and it feels so good I let out a little moan. Just as I start to really enjoy it, I feel a sharp sting as his heavy hand cracks down on my right cheek.

I've never been spanked before and I'm not sure what to make of it. My skin tingles a bit with a slight pain, but it doesn't hurt, not really. I'm more aroused by the fact that I'm lying across Drew's lap and I can feel his huge cock beneath me.

"Is tha—" I start to say when I feel another smack, this time on my left cheek. I'm still not sure if I liked it or not, but I do know I felt my pussy clench that time. Before I have time to think, I receive two more smacks on each cheek, forcing me to moan in pleasure.

"There it is. You want more?" I don't answer because I'm not sure. I've never done this before, so I really don't know. "I think you do, but you need to speak up." He spanks me again on each side and I can tell he's being careful not to hit in the same place.

Petting the heated skin, he says, "You need to tell me what you like, Liss. How you like it. I'm going to be your man and I need to know. I'll just keep spanking you until you tell me."

"I… um… well, I—" Smack, smack, smack. Three more spanks, this time a little harder, but still pleasurable. My pussy flutters as my juices drip down my legs. *I think I'm gonna come.*

Soothing the skin, he demands, "Tell me, Liss. I

wanna know what you like. How do you want me to fuck you, baby? I need to know what you want."

"I-I… I don't know—" Smack, smack. Two more spanks. This feels so good, but I'm trying to tell him. I really am, but my senses are so overwhelmed right now I can barely focus.

"Why won't you tell me, baby? You don't want me to fuck you? You just wanna be spanked? I can go all night like this, but your ass is gonna be raw tomorrow, Liss."

"Please! I… I can't… tell you what I like because I don't know!" I'm practically yelling at this point. The spanking feels so good I can barely stand it. But I'm on edge and I'm aching and throbbing, and the need to come is almost unbearable.

He jerks me up off his lap so he can look me in the eyes. He holds my gaze and I'm almost on the verge of tears, afraid of what he sees and worried he might change his mind if he knows the truth. Whatever he's looking for within my eyes, he must find it, because a slow smile begins to spread across his face.

"Why don't you know, baby? Dear God, are you telling me you're a virgin?" I drop my head in embarrassment, but he catches my chin with his finger and lifts my head. "You have nothing to be embarrassed about. This is the greatest fucking gift I've ever received, Liss."

"You still want me?" I whisper.

"Fucking yes, I want you. I told you, you're mine. This just makes it even sweeter." He grabs my hand

and pulls me up. "Come on. We're going to my bedroom where I can fuck you all night." I'm not about to argue with that.

He pulls me along behind him, the two of us practically running down the hall like teenagers. We're both aching with need and if we can hold out just a little bit longer, it's going to be the sweetest release either of us has ever experienced.

CHAPTER 7

DREW

I don't know what I did to have this girl, but I don't fucking deserve her. Elissa is a wet fucking dream come to life and she's all mine. *Mine!* I'll never let her go and nothing and no one will ever take her away from me.

How she's still a virgin is some kind of miracle. She's the most beautiful woman I've ever seen and I know I'm not the only one who thinks so. Every man at the restaurant tonight turned and looked at my girl. Each one of those bastards wanted her and she was there with me. I'm the luckiest asshole of all because she's all mine.

I've never been so turned on in my damn life. The feel of her hot skin against my hand as I spanked her ass, watching the flesh bounce with each smack... When I saw how red her flesh became, and smelled her sweet arousal as it dripped from her pussy, I almost came in my pants. I wanted to fall to my knees behind her and lick up every fucking drop.

Knowing no man has ever done that to her before is the sweetest thing I've ever heard. The best gift I'll ever receive is knowing her tight pink pussy will only ever be touched by me. I can't wait to get my hands, my mouth, my dick, and my cum all fucking over her pussy.

I lead her into my dark room and shut the door. "Lights, twenty percent," I call out to the automated system. A soft glow illuminates us and I see her standing before me, a nervous expression covering her face.

"Make no mistake, I am going to fuck you, Liss. But I promise to make it good for you and I promise you'll like it," I tell her as I walk towards her, grabbing her waist and pulling her body into mine.

"I trust you, Drew," she says in a husky voice.

I spin her around and unzip her dress. Kissing her skin as it becomes exposed, I slide the material off her body and let it fall to the floor. I deftly remove her strapless bra and leave her completely naked, facing away from me.

"Turn around, baby." She's nervous and I can see her pulse jumping wildly at the base of her neck. Her full tits gently sway with her quick breaths. If she bites that pillowy lower lip of hers any harder, I'm afraid it'll bleed. I slowly rake my eyes up and down her body, forcing her to endure my stare.

"You're fucking gorgeous, Elissa. Every damn inch of you is sheer perfection. There isn't a place on your body that I'm not gonna touch or kiss or suck or lick tonight. Do you understand?" She nods. "Words, Liss."

"Yes, Drew."

"Good girl. Undress me, baby." She steps forward, her shaky hands reaching for me. I capture her fingertips and bring them to my lips, kissing them softly. Letting go, I drop my hands to my sides and allow her to do as I've asked.

Having already shucked my jacket back in the sitting room, she begins unbuttoning my shirt at a painfully slow pace—every few seconds, looking up at me to gage my reaction. Seeing that I'm enjoying what she's doing, she gains confidence and becomes more certain of her actions. She glides her hands over my abs and pecs several times before she pushes my shirt over my shoulders and down my arms, until it falls to the floor.

She takes a moment to admire my body and I feel like a fucking king, knowing she's impressed with how well I take care of myself. Leaning down, she presses gentle kisses to my heated skin as her hands roam all over my torso. Every fiber of my being tells me to take over and take control, but I know this is her first time and that she's never been with a man before. Pushing down my bastard tendencies, I force myself to be perfectly still and let her explore my body as she pleases.

I feel her warm breath as she opens her mouth, followed by the wet tip of her tongue as she licks my nipple. A zing of pleasure spikes through me all the way down to my dick and the fucker jerks in response against her belly. Her eyes snap up to mine in questioning curiosity.

"My dick likes it when you do that, baby. But I'm hanging on by a thread here. I know this is your first time, but maybe we can explore later after I fuck you senseless." I see her abs contract when I say that and I know she just clenched her core. "Take off my pants so I can fuck you."

She unbuckles and removes my belt, then pops the button and unzips my slacks. Taking a step even closer, Elissa hooks her thumbs into the waistband of my pants and boxer briefs, sliding them over my ass and down my thighs. They fall the rest of the way to the floor and I kick them off before removing my socks and tossing them into the pile of clothes.

My long, thick cock is so hard it bounces between us, precum dripping from the tip and onto the floor. Her eyes widen as she stares at it, licking her lips like she wants a taste. She reaches out to touch it, but I know if she does, I'll lose all control so I stop her and take over the situation.

"Get on the bed, baby. I need to get you ready."

"O-oh. Okay." She turns and walks to the bed, her luscious ass swaying as she goes.

"On your back, feet planted on the bed, legs spread for me." Like a good girl, she does as I asked, and I walk around to the front of the bed so I can get the best view.

Seeing Elissa in the middle of my bed, spread open for me, is the most beautiful sight I've ever seen.

Her gorgeous pussy is like a chocolate-covered strawberry, her bare lips opening up to her juicy pink core.

Fuck, she's wet.

I can see her honey dripping from her pussy down to the rosette of her ass and onto the sheets. I bet she tastes as sweet as she looks and I'm going to find out right fucking now.

Climbing on to the bed, I wedge my shoulder between her thighs and frame her pussy with my hands. I look up at her to see her watching me, her eyes hooded with lust.

"Has anyone ever licked this pussy before, baby?"

"No, no one," she says, her tits so big I almost can't see her.

"Good, and no one besides me will ever get a taste either." I close my eyes and deeply inhale the sweet scent of her arousal. *Damn, she smells fucking good!* Opening my eyes, I pull back her lips with my thumbs and take a long, languid lick from bottom to top with my flattened tongue, flicking my tip across her clit. Her loud moan is fucking music to my ears.

I do it again and again, like I'm eating an ice cream cone on a hot day, and her hips start to roll with me. I begin to devour her pussy in earnest, covering her with my mouth and eating at her voraciously. Her hands begin clawing at the sheets and I start teasing her hole with the tip of my finger.

When more of her honey begins to spill from her pussy, I slide my finger into her tight core, curling it gently to loosen her up. Her moans get louder and I take it as a sign she's ready for me to add another finger. I scissor my two digits in the tight space, knowing if I don't, she'll never be able to take my fat cock. Once I start flicking her clit with the tip of my tongue and rubbing her G-spot, I know she's ready to come for me.

"Drew! Oh, God! I'm coming!"

"I know, baby. Let go. Give it to me." I double down on my ministrations and a few seconds later, she explodes in my mouth, filling it with her juices that I gladly swallow down. Lapping up every fucking drop, I lick her clean, but I continue to petting her pretty pussy, knowing I need to keep her wet to take my dick.

Eventually her hands release the sheets and she brings them to her chest as she catches her breath. I climb over her body, kissing my way up as I go until I reach her mouth. I kiss her deeply, letting her taste her cream again, which I know she likes and turns her on.

Instinctively, she wraps her legs around me as her hands cup my face while we kiss. I finger fuck her pussy as she rides my hand, her body quickly learning naturally what to do. The sounds of her soaking wet pussy fill the room and I know she's as ready as she'll ever be to take my dick.

I nibble her lower lip before breaking away from the kiss. I give her a wink then reach over to the nightstand to grab a condom. Just as I almost get my hands on the drawer, Elissa grabs my wrist and stops me.

"I'm on the pill, Drew. And I'm clean. I've never been with anyone. Are… are you… I mean…"

"I've never had sex without a condom in my life, Elissa. And I'm clean. I'm regularly tested."

"Oh. We can use a condom. I just thought…" I inadvertently let out a growl.

"Fuck that. You're fucking mine, Liss. And if you trust me, I'm fucking my girl bare. I don't want anything between us. Ever." I slam my mouth down on hers and kiss her stupid. She's grinding her hips against me while I mouth-fuck her and I know it's time to claim my girl.

I slip the head of my cock through her wetness a few times, loving the sloppy sounds as well as the moans she makes each time I rub against her clit. Notching at her entrance, I make sure her eyes are on me. When she nods, I do my best to rein in my control and slide in slowly, inch by inch, knowing I'm stretching her tight pussy.

Her eyes narrow in pain, but my girl forces them to stay open and trained on mine. When I reach the thin barrier of her innocence, I lean down and kiss the fuck out of her to distract her. I pull out slightly then slide back in, going all the way to the hilt, until my balls are flush against her ass.

She cries out in pain, but I stay perfectly still, giving her time to adjust to my size, and let the sting of the stretch fade away. I kiss her neck and her tits, sucking on her nipples, licking and nibbling at her until her arousal grows again. When I feel her hips move, I know she's ready and I take her mouth in another kiss.

I start out slow, thrusting in and out, in and out—long, smooth strokes that rub her sweet spot each time. Her head thrashes back and forth in pleasure and a fine sheen of sweat begins to break out on both of our bodies. Picking up my pace, I begin to fuck her a little faster, but I'm careful not to give her more than she can handle. I'm a bastard, but I'll never do anything to hurt my girl.

"You're holding back from me, Drew. I can feel it."

"I'm not that big of an asshole, Liss. I'm trying not to hurt you."

"I've waited my whole life for you. Now, fuck me like you promised," she says, and damn it if there isn't fire in my girl's eyes. *Fuck, this girl is mine.*

Giving in to the primal need I have inside me, I start to fuck her with wild abandon. I lift one leg over my shoulder and wrap the other around my waist, pulling her hips slightly up at an angle that allows me to get even deeper. As I pump into her hard and fast, our bodies are slapping together, the smell of sex filling the room.

I hold onto her leg that's on my shoulder and I rub her clit with my other hand. With each sharp thrust, her tits bounce and it turns me on even more. I command her, "Play with your tits while I make you come." She immediately grabs onto the large round globes and massages them, pulling on them and pinching her nipples.

My dick jerks at the sight as precum leaks from my tip. I rub her clit harder and her pussy walls clamp down tight when she comes on my cock, screaming my name like the sweetest prayer. I don't give her any time to recover, flipping her over instead, before pushing her face down onto the bed and pulling her hips up to meet mine.

I slam my cock hard into her dripping wet pussy while my thumb presses against the tight rosette of her ass. I'm not going to take her there today, but soon. I'm going to claim every hole my girl has and she will belong to me in every way. Pressing my thumb a bit harder as I fuck her roughly from behind, I watch as more of her honey drips down my dick and my balls and I know without a doubt, this girl was fucking made to be mine.

"Tell me you're close, Liss. 'Cause I'm about to fill you up with all my cum, baby."

"Yes, yes. Come with me. I want you to come inside me, Drew," she whines.

I ram my cock into her a few more times, her flesh rippling from the force of each thrust. After three more pumps, we both explode, her pussy squeezing me in a vice-like grip that's so tight I think it might break my dick. My vision becomes dark and hazy as jet after jet of hot creamy cum paints the inside of her womb. I've never come so hard or so much in my life, and all I can think about is the day when I can fuck my baby into her and see her pregnant with our child.

Elissa collapses on the bed, pulling her tight core off my dick much too soon. I lie down next to her and tug her sated and exhausted body against mine, tangling our legs together before resting her head on my chest.

"You don't ever get to leave me, Elissa. You're mine, now."

"As long as you know you're mine too," she says sleepily.

"Damn right, I am," I tell her. Her leg is tossed over mine and I reach down to her pussy, pushing the cum that's seeping out back inside her, where it belongs.

I've done what I wanted to do and I've made Elissa mine now. But I'm just as much hers. There is no way in hell I'm ever letting her go.

CHAPTER 8

DREW

I normally use Sundays to prep for the work week, but today for once in my life, I actually slept in. It couldn't be helped though—Elissa wore me the fuck out. My woman is fucking insatiable. *Who knew once I took her virginity, she'd demand my dick every five minutes?* I'm not complaining, though. Yeah, my dick is fucking sore as hell, but being inside her sweet pussy is nothing but the purest heaven.

After wearing her out Friday night, I made sure to take care of her Saturday morning. I knew she'd be sore and needed a break so I gave her a good soak in the tub before taking her around the city for some sightseeing. After a quiet dinner at home, we fucked each other to sleep, each of us reaching for the other throughout the night to satisfy our need for more orgasms.

I woke her up this morning with my mouth on her pussy before I fucked her to sleep again. Now I'm serving her brunch in bed, so we can at least make ourselves presentable before her brother arrives. That's a conversation I'm not looking forward to.

Elissa already messaged her boss, Matt, and let him know she's taking the job. Of course, with the job comes paid relocation expenses for an apartment, which she said she'd take. I made sure to let her know that not only would I spank her ass red, but over my dead body would my woman be living anywhere else other than with me.

The only person left to handle is Thomas. She wants to talk to him herself, but no way in hell am I letting her do that on her own. And we're not even going to do it together. I'm her man, and I'm going to take care of it. Besides, Thomas is my best friend. He trusted me to take care of his sister and he needs to know that's exactly what I'm doing.

I put the glass of orange juice on the tray, along with the mug of coffee that's fixed with cream and sugar, just the way she likes it. This morning, I made her an omelet and fresh fruit since we had such a heavy dinner last night. Carefully carrying the tray, I walk down the hall and into our bedroom, where I find her still sleeping on our bed. *"Our bed." That'll never get old.*

"Wake up, baby. Your brother will be here soon," I say, sitting on the opposite side of the bed before setting the tray down where she can see it. She flutters open her eyes and gives me a sleepy smile. *God, she's beautiful.*

"Did you make me breakfast?"

"Yep. Never done this shit before, so I hope it's alright," I tell her, and it's true. I've never had women over to my penthouse, refusing to bring them here. And I damn sure never stayed the night with one. This is all new to me, but it somehow feels right with Elissa. I feel this innate desire to own her, protect her, provide for her, take care of her… love her.

"It's perfect. Thank you, Drew," she says sweetly, sitting up and pulling the sheet to cover her bare chest. Unable to resist, I crawl over to her on my belly and tug the sheet down, sucking one of her nipples into my hot, wet mouth. Arching her back in pleasure, she inadvertently forces more of her soft mound in my face and I relish the feel of her smooth skin.

Pulling off her nipple with an audible pop, I tell her, "Eat your breakfast, baby. I'm gonna shower and get ready. When you're finished, come find me in my office."

"Okay." I get off the bed and lean down to steal a kiss. I only mean for it to be a chaste one, but she captures my face between her hands, holding me captive as she licks the seam of my lips asking for entry. Not one to deny my girl, I open for her but immediately take control. I kiss her passionately until we're both a little dizzy. When she moans softly, I know I have to stop, or we'll never leave this room.

Pulling away, I say, "Stop trying to tempt me, woman. Eat your breakfast."

"Spoilsport."

"Behave and I'll reward you later." I quickly kiss her nose and practically run into the bathroom to get ready before I say "fuck it" and spend all day in bed with her instead. *This woman is gonna be the death of me.*

* * *

"Hey, man. Wow, are you slumming it today?" Thomas asks, walking into the penthouse. I heard the chime signaling that someone was coming up the elevator. Confirming it was him on the security camera, I went to meet him at the door.

"What do you mean?"

"I mean, Sunday is practically just another workday to you, but here you are in sweats. Are you sick or something? Where's Liss?" I intentionally ignore his question.

"You want a drink or something? What time did you get in?" I ask him.

"I got back last night. Where's Liss? I don't see her suitcase. Is she ready?"

"Have a seat, man. Let's catch up." He narrows his eyes at me, but doesn't say anything. We walk into the sitting room, both of us taking a seat. Last I checked, Liss was taking a shower, so hopefully Thomas and I can hash this out before she comes out here.

"What's up, Drew? What the fuck is going on?" He sits back on the sofa and crosses his arms over his chest. Thomas is a big guy, about as big as I am. He was a linebacker in high school, but only played recreationally in college. Still, he hits the gym daily and at 6'3" and over 200 pounds of solid muscle, he's no one to toy with.

"Liss is fine, man. Calm down," I say, raising my hands in a placating manner.

"Well, you're freaking me the fuck out. I know you better than anybody and I know you got something to say. So, spit it out already." Thomas is my CFO and he's usually all finance and finesse. He's as smooth as silk and he knows how to massage business deals for me. But right now, he's Thomas Jones—Elissa's big brother and ass kicker of anyone who hurts her.

"Fuck, man. Fine. You're my best friend. Remember that, okay." He gives me a hard ass look that says, *Get on with it, motherfucker*. "Liss canceled her flight. She took the job and she isn't going back."

"Okay. Well, that's great. That's a promotion for her, right? Alright, cool. She can just stay with me until she finds a place." He has a confused look on his face, like he can't understand why I'm making this such a big deal. And damn, if I'm not dreading this next part.

"She's not staying with you, man. She's staying with me."

"WHAT THE FUCK?!" His voice booms loudly from the vaulted ceilings as he stands abruptly, his hands balled into fists at his sides.

"Calm. The. Fuck. Down," I say quietly through clenched teeth. "Sit down, man."

"I fucking trusted you! What the fuck did you do?!" He starts pacing back and forth. "She's not staying here. Where is she?" I stand up so we're eye to eye.

"She's not going anywhere. She belongs here with me."

"What the fuck is that supposed to mean, Drew? Did you fuck my sister?!"

"Watch your fucking mouth when you talk about my woman," I tell him, giving him a deadly fucking glare.

"Oh, that's fucking rich. 'Your woman'? You don't date, Drew! Did you forget I've known you for the last decade? You don't even let them come to your penthouse, man. You never see them more than once. You use them and you throw them the fuck away. You're not gonna do that to Elissa. I won't let you hurt her."

"You're right... you do know me better than anyone. And yeah, before her, I did only do one-night-stands. But she's it for me. I can't explain it... it just is. And you fucking know me—I take care of what's mine. Elissa is mine, Thomas. She's fucking mine."

"You're just gonna break her heart, man. You just met her. You don't even know her."

"I swear I will never hurt her. I thought you trusted me with everything?" I ask him.

"I've never had to trust you with anything this important or this valuable before. This is my baby sister, Drew. There is nothing more important or more valuable than her."

"I know that and I agree with you. I love her, Thomas. I don't know what to say, man. It's only been a few days, but she's turned my life upside down and I fucking love her." Frustrated, I run my hands through my hair, wondering what I can say to get my best friend to understand there is nothing in this world that will make me give Elissa up or let her walk away from me.

"You do?" I hear Elissa's soft, angelic voice ask from off to my left. Thomas and I both snap our heads in her direction. My strides quickly eat up the floor that separates us as I make my way to her.

"Yes, I do. You should have been the first one to hear it, but as you can see, your brother and I were in a bit of a heated discussion." I wrap my arms around her and pull her into a warm embrace. "I love you, Liss," I say, kissing the top of her head.

She looks up at me, her eyes shining with unshed tears, and she says, "I love you, too." I slant my mouth to hers and kiss her with everything I've got, showing her that even though it's only been a few days since she burst into my life, she means everything to me and I'll never let her go. The sound of a throat clearing reminds us we're not alone.

"I still think I should kick your ass," Thomas says, his beefy arms crossed over his chest and stretching the cuffs of his sleeves on his t-shirt.

"But I'm hoping that as your best friend, you won't." He walks over to us, and drags Elissa away from me, making me growl at him. Elissa laughs as he pulls her into a bear hug.

"And you're happy, Lissa Bear?"

"I'm happy, Tommy Bear," she says, wrapping her arms around his muscular body as tightly as she can.

"Tommy Bear, huh?" I smirk at him.

"Shut the hell up," he responds, glaring at me. "If you ever hurt my sister, so help me, I will fuck you up." He points a thick finger in my direction.

"Never, man. I'll always take care of her," I say, pulling her back into my arms. I can't believe I didn't even want to meet this girl… now she's mine forever.

EPILOGUE

ELISSA
One Year Later

SOME DAYS, I CAN'T BELIEVE THIS IS ACTUALLY my life. I feel like I'm living in a fairytale with my own happily ever after, just like one of the many books I love to read. But my Prince Charming isn't so much a prince, but rather he's a growly alpha sex-god who fucks like a demon. None the less, he's all mine and there's no one else I'd rather belong to.

Now I have my dream editing job at an awesome publishing company. I live in the most amazing penthouse with views of almost the entire city. I live near my brother, who I get to see on a regular basis instead of just at the holidays. And Drew Cohen is the most perfect husband a girl could ask for.

Part of me was surprised when Drew proposed after only three months. But then again, I wasn't because we were instantly in love and living together since the first weekend we met. He actually would have proposed a month sooner, but it took that long to have my engagement ring made, since he had it custom-designed with a halo, antique, emerald-cut pink diamond. I told him it was too much, but then again, he's a billionaire so what did I really expect from Mr. Extravagant?

I'm not used to such lavish things so he promised me a small wedding. True to his word, we had just that. But I should have been more specific. Yes, the wedding was small, with only one hundred and fifty guests, but we were treated to an all-expenses-paid destination wedding in the Maldives. Like I said, my life is a fairytale, but who am I to complain?

I hear the melodic chime overhead and check the time on my laptop. It's just after five o'clock and I smile because I know it took some effort for Drew to come home at this hour. He's been doing better, especially now that we're married and want to start a family, but I know it's hard for him to wrap up and leave the office before six-thirty.

I finish editing this last paragraph, before saving my work and shutting down my laptop. I have my own office down at corporate, which isn't far from here, but sometimes I like to do some extra edits at home—where it's quiet and I can work sitting by my floor-to-ceiling windows, overlooking the city. I'm just closing my computer, when I hear Drew's dress shoes on the floor as he walks towards me.

"I knew I'd find you here." He leans down and places a kiss on the top of my head. I look up and smile at him.

"How was work, babe?"

"Good, we're acquiring another small start-up company, so I'm sending your brother out of town."

"Can't you send someone else? He's never gonna date anyone, if you keep making him travel," I say, standing up and wrapping my arms around my gorgeous husband.

"Yeah, 'cause that's why he's not dating." He smirks at me.

"Well, you're not helping the situation."

"Leave the man alone, Liss. He'll date when he's ready."

"Is that so?" I say, putting my hands on my hips.

"Are you sassing me, woman?" He quirks an eyebrow at me. I don't answer because I know exactly where this is leading and it's just where I want it to go. Instead, I quirk an eyebrow right back at him. "I see. My girl wants to play." He makes a tsking sound with his tongue. *I've waited all day for this.*

He takes off his suit jacket and lays it over the arm of the chair. Never taking his eyes off mine, he loosens his tie before removing it from his neck. He walks over to me as I stand by the window and lifts the hem of my dress. When his hand cups my bare pussy he sucks in a breath between his clenched teeth.

"Hmmm... no panties today. And you sassed me.

How many spanks should you get for that?" he says, leaning in to leave open-mouth kisses on my neck while his finger slides through my dripping wet slit.

"Let's start with five," I answer in a husky voice.

"Good girl. Take your dress off and put your hands on the glass, Liss." My whole body shudders with anticipation.

I do as my sexy husband commands, thinking to myself that I'm the luckiest girl in the whole world—I'm living a smutty romance fantasy and it's absolutely perfect.

THE END

THANK YOU!

From the bottom of my heart, thank you for reading my book! I'm just a true Southern girl, living with my amazing hubby and my princess diva baby girl, reading and writing books, asking you to love me. I hope my mix of romance, with a dash of swoon, and a pinch of smut brings a smile to your face and a tingle to your fun bits.

If you enjoyed my book, please consider leaving a review on Amazon, Goodreads, etc. Even if it's just a sentence or two about what you liked most about my book, it will help my work to be seen by other readers.

HAPPY READING!

FIND ELYSE KELLY

EMAIL
elyse@elysekellybooks.com

AMAZON
www.amazon.com/author/elysekelly

GOODREADS
www.goodreads.com/elysekelly

INSTAGRAM
www.instagram.com/authorelysekelly

FACEBOOK
www.facebook.com/authorelysekelly

Sign up for my newsletter to receive updates about upcoming releases, exclusives giveaways, and more! And you'll receive a FREE COPY of my novella WANTING MY BEST FRIEND!
eepurl.com/hgMKmT

ACKNOWLEDGEMENTS

To my amazing family, thank you for supporting me and each and every passion I've wanted to pursue. You always encourage me to do whatever makes me happy and I'm so grateful to have you all. I love you and I hope I make you proud each and every day.

To my author friends who provide invaluable advice and an offer to be my sounding board, thanks for EVERYTHING! I would never have been brave enough to pursue my passion without you, and I would have no clue what I'm doing without your help along the way.

To Sarah, thanks for being daily dose of sanity. Not only are we on this bookish journey together, but you're bestest bestie I've never met! Love you, girl!

To Michelle, Nisha, and Kat, thanks for helping me make this the most amazing manuscript for my readers! You guys not only help me make my books better, but your support is beyond anything I could have ever expected.

To all the readers, bookstagrammers, and bloggers, thank you for reading, reviewing, and promoting my books. I wouldn't be here without you and I'm so thankful for each and every one of you.

Turn the page for a sneak peek at

The Sweet Spot
Magnolia Springs Book 1

Available now through Amazon and
free in Kindle Unlimited!

THE SWEET SPOT
Magnolia Springs Book 1

ELYSE KELLY

Copyright © 2020 Elyse Kelly
All rights reserved.
ISBN: 9798685473103

Cover Design: Sarah Kil Creative Studio
Editing: Pagan Proofreading

The unauthorized reproduction, transmission, or distribution of any part of this copyrighted work is illegal. No part of this book may be reproduced in any form or by any means without the express written permission from the author, except for the use of brief quotations in a book review.

This literary work is fiction. Any resemblance to actual persons, living or dead, events, or establishments is entirely coincidental.

CHAPTER 1

CALLIE

It's finally happening! I can't believe it's finally happening! This is legit my life right now! Holy shit, I'm so excited!

When I told my parents I was moving to Georgia, they both looked at me like I sprouted a magic unicorn horn and pink hooves. They've always known I wanted to open my own specialty bakery and they have been the most supportive parents a girl could ask for. They just thought I wanted to open my bakery in our hometown in Tennessee. I never mentioned moving and I certainly didn't mention moving so far away.

I lived out of state for a few years when I went to culinary school, but ever the good daughter, I came home monthly and promptly moved back right after graduation. I've been working at a bakery back home for two years, learning the ropes and saving my money. But now it's time for this baby bird to leave the nest. I hate to leave my parents, but I'm ready to start my own life and I'm ready to do it in another town. *Deuces!*

So here I am! Finally living in Magnolia Springs, Georgia, just outside of Savannah and I. LOVE. IT! This is the cutest town EVER! I feel like I'm living in one of those made-for-TV romance movies. It's a small town with only about 20,000 people, but it's perfect. Everywhere you turn there's a smiling face. You can drive down any street and someone will wave at you as you go by. Everyone speaks to you, even if they don't know you. And there's even a Main Street with cute shops and boutiques, family-owned businesses, and now a cupcake shop. *You're welcome, Magnolia Springs!*

I'm about a week out from the grand opening of The Sweet Spot. Somehow, I convinced my bestie Ava to move with me and help me open the bakery. I don't think this is exactly what she planned to do with her life, but she loves me and I could tell she was running away from something back home. Though I'm not sure what that something is, at some point, I'll get to the bottom it. Ava has been my BFF since kindergarten and there is no way I could live without her. So, when I saw she needed to get away, I dragged her with me to open The Sweet Spot.

I've only been in town for a few weeks, getting the shop ready, and settling in to our cozy little home. Today I'm working on promoting our grand opening, so I've whipped up some cupcakes to take to the other businesses on Main Street. There's a mechanic's shop on the left side of my bakery, and a trendy clothing boutique to the right. There're other businesses as you go down the street, so I'll try to hit those up later today, too. Far be it from me to deny anyone a chance to get free cupcakes.

Sophie's is the cutest boutique I think I've ever set foot in. The clothes are amazing and there's also little trinkets, gifts, home goods, and a ton of other stuff. You can tell this is the kind of place someone has poured a lot of time and love into. You can't help but feel happy as soon as you walk in. The front door chimes softly as I open it, signaling my entrance.

"Hi, there! I'll be with you in just a sec." I hear called from somewhere in the store.

"No worries. Take your time." I take a look around, being careful not to drop the box of a dozen cupcakes I'm holding. Ava would love this place. We'll definitely be back here soon to drop some cash. Gotta support local businesses! After a few minutes, I hear someone approaching me.

"Hi, I'm Sophie. I think I've seen you around. You're new in town, right?" Sophie looks to be about my age. She's beautiful, with milk chocolate hair and striking green eyes. I'd kill for her complexion. She looks very boho chic, but in an effortless way—kind of like Stevie Nicks. She's dressed in a high-waisted hi-lo skirt that ties at the middle and a simple baby pink t-shirt tucked into it.

"Yeah, I'm Callie. I'm opening The Sweet Spot next door. I hope we haven't disturbed you too much with our remodeling the last few weeks."

"Not at all. I'm happy to see someone moving in, now that the Johnsons have retired and moved to Florida."

"Well, I hope you like cupcakes because these are for you. Our grand opening is this Saturday so I thought I'd bribe you to come check out my shop, with some awesome goodness right here."

"You had me at cupcakes!" she says with widened eyes. I open the box to let her see how amazeballs I am at baking cupcakes. Yeah, that's right, I'm not afraid to toot my own horn!

"These smell like unicorn dreams and rainbows!" I think she's actually drooling now. I try not to stare as she's eye-fucking my cupcakes like she's thinking dirty thoughts. Hell, I don't know this girl. Maybe she *is* thinking dirty thoughts. *You do you, girl!*

"Uh… should I maybe give you some alone time with those?"

"Gah! Sorry! Didn't mean to be so awkward. These just look and smell so amazing that I had a moment of insanity. Thanks for bringing these by! I can't wait to try them!"

"I hope you like them. And maybe you could

mention to your customers there's an awesome new cupcake bakery opening next door?" I ask hesitantly as I clasp my hands behind my back and dig the toe of my converse into the floor.

"Oh, you got it! I'm excited to see someone my own age around here. I grew up here and a lot of kids move away for college and don't come back. The town's mostly parents and grandparents, and nosy ol' busy-bodies that stay all up in your business. It's quiet and low-key around here, but there are no secrets safe in Magnolia Springs. Just keep that in mind.

"Truth be told, I've known about you since the day you got here. The gossips in town couldn't wait to tell everyone about the new girl. And apparently you have a roommate? You guys are renting the Watson's house on Dogwood, right?"

"Well shit, I guess there really are no secrets here. My bestie Ava and I moved here from Tennessee about six weeks ago."

"Oh, I know. Like I said, no secrets. But don't worry, you'll love it here. Everyone is super nice, even if they are a bit nosy and gossipy. Just steer clear of Stacy Trent and her Misfit Toys. They're our age but still living in their high school days, wearing pink on Wednesdays and thinking life is the extended cut of Mean Girls. A gorgeous girl like you will definitely be on their radar."

"Thanks for the heads up. I've known my fair share of mean girls, so I think I can handle 'em. Well, I've got another delivery to make. I hope we can hang out soon. I could always use a new friend in town." She claps her hands and jumps up and down like she's on *The Price is Right*.

"Yes! I'll definitely be your Magnolia Springs tour guide!" I grin at her, thinking to myself, "This girl is too much." I give her a quick hug, 'cause I'm a hugger, and tell her I'll see her soon. I make my way back to the shop to pick up another box of cupcakes to deliver to the auto shop next door. If they're half as friendly as Sophie, I know I've made the right decision to move here.

CHAPTER 2

ASHER

I just wrapped up putting a new alternator on the Honda Odyssey minivan Mrs. Smith dropped off this morning. I don't know how she manages with five kids, but if I can help keep her moving while she carts around her own personal basketball team, it's the least I could do. Her husband works out of town a lot, so she's definitely got her hands full with those hellions of hers.

I wipe my greasy hands on the rag I keep in my back pocket and smooth my hair off my face before replacing my favorite hat backwards on my head. I walk out to the front of the shop to write the ticket for Mrs. Smith, but I stop dead in my tracks just before I open the glass door that separates the front office from the body shop.

Well, fuck me to the moon and back! Who is SHE?! I quickly close my gaping mouth as my dick begins to tingle before I open the door to find out who this goddess is. She hasn't noticed me yet, so I take a moment to appreciate the girl in front of me, as she's looking around my lobby, unaware of my presence. She has the most beautiful, light caramel skin with long, curly black hair that I bet would feel so soft wrapped up in my fist. Curves for days and an hour-glass figure that makes me wanna drop to my knees and motorboat her tits. Her banging body is all woman with an ass that puts a Kardashian to shame. My favorite part though, is that she's dressed in a vintage Weezer t-shirt, dark blue skinny jeans that look painted on her luscious body, and black converse on her cute little feet. *It's about to be on like Donkey Kong!*

Just as I get ready to open the door to the woman of my dreams, a hand claps me on my shoulder. My best friend, Dane, who works at the shop with me and my brother Christian, lets out a low whistle and asks, "Where's she been all my life?" Before I can think straight, I shuck off his huge hand and blurt out, "Mine!" Then quickly I open the door. I walk toward the front desk with Dane hot on my heels, chuckling under his breath and shaking his head at me. She turns to me and Dane, holding a hot pink box in her hands like it contains a prized possession.

"Hi, I'm Callie!" she says brightly, in a voice that could only come from an angel. Dane is quick to reach out from where he's standing behind me and offer his hand.

"I'm in love!" Dane tells her with a smile. "I'm Dane,

by the way. And this is Asher." She giggles softly as her cheeks turn a soft peach flush. Damn, is that sexy! And she's not even trying.

"I'm Asher," I say like an idiot. Shaking my head, I inwardly cringe. *Real smooth, Asher, real smooth.*

She smiles at me sweetly. "So, he said. Here, these are for you." I take the box from her hands and open it to see the most mouth-watering cupcakes I've ever seen. Each one, a different flavor with mile high frosting on top.

"You wanna be my wife?" Dane says to her as he drools over the cupcakes from over my shoulder.

I nudge him in the ribs. "These are mine and I'm not sharing." He gives me a mock affronted look and pouts. "But I'm your best friend!"

"Now now, boys, sharing is caring," she chastises us jokingly. She winks at me and my dick that I willed to calm down earlier is now trying his damnedest to get to her. She looks at me with these soul-stealing, sterling silver eyes and I know I've got to get it together before I fall all over her. *You're better than this, Asher!*

"My cupcake shop, The Sweet Spot, opens next week. Our grand opening is Saturday. We're neighbors!" I can't take my eyes off her lips as she's speaking.

"So… can I bribe you guys with these cupcakes and get you to come to the grand opening? Maybe tell all your customers about my new place?" she says, looking up at me through her long, black lashes.

"I'll be there on one condition." I give her my best mega-watt smile. She may be new in town, and maybe she's affecting my dick more than any woman ever has before, but I'm Asher Davis. No woman has ever said no to this smile and these dimples. I cock my head to the side and look deep in her eyes, "Go out with me."

That sweet peach blush is back and she bites her pillowy lower lip, but then she gives her head a subtle shake like she's clearing a fog from her brain.

"Hmmmm… maybe another time."

"Damn, son! That has never happened before!" Dane says exactly what I'm thinking, covering his mouth with his fist and laughing behind me. Maybe she misunderstood me. Right? *Who would turn down these dimples?*

"What's that now?" I ask her surprised, my eyebrows almost at my hairline.

"I just have a lot on my plate, opening the bakery right now." She lifts her shoulder in a slight shrug. Gaining conviction, she says, "And besides, you have 'heart-breaker', 'panty-melter', and 'trouble-maker' written all over you. My mama told me all about boys like you." She quirks her eyebrow, daring me to tell her it's not true. So, what if it's true? She doesn't know that. Yet.

"And just what did your mama say about boys like me?"

"Wouldn't you like to know," she says. "I've got to get going. It was nice to meet you. See ya, boys! Enjoy the cupcakes! They taste as sweet as they look." With a parting wink, the little minx sways her sweet hips right out the front door.

"I'm giving you one chance with that girl, before I'm all over that." I cut my eyes at Dane and punch him in the arm, letting him know that little Miss Callie is all mine.

A second later the front door chimes and Christian walks in, letting out a loud wolf whistle. "Did you guys catch the hottie outside?"

"Mine!" I say, like some kind of caveman that wants to club her over the head and drag her back to my cave. I don't know what it is about this girl that's gotten my full attention, but she has it. And I'm not settling for a no.

Okay, my little cupcake. You wanna play hard to get? Well, game on, baby. I love a good chase.

CHAPTER 3

CALLIE

I. AM. SCREWED! I can't squeeze my thighs together tight enough to relieve the sexual tension I'm feeling in my lady bits right now. That man is sex on a stick! Walking, talking, breathing sex. Sweet mama, am I in trouble.

That is the most gorgeous man I've ever seen. So tall and muscular, his body lean and built from hours of physical labor. Thick dark hair pulled back under a backwards hat. Cerulean blue eyes that demand your attention. And those dimples! That man definitely leaves a wake of exploded ovaries everywhere he goes.

And his friend Dane is just as hot! Gotta be over six and a half feet of sexy chocolate, and built like a Mack truck with muscles on top of muscles. Black hair close-cropped, with scruff that begs to be rubbed against a woman's bare skin, and a smile that drops panties within seconds.

Then I almost run over hottie number three when

I walked out the door. He looked a lot like Asher, but with blond hair and no dimples. I'd bet they were brothers with how similar they look. He had a sexy swagger about him too, as he came strutting through the door. *What are they putting in the water here?!* Those three boys are nothing but living, breathing sex gods!

I barrel into The Sweet Spot and quickly lock up. I've gotta get away from all that sexiness before my ovaries faint! I close the back door and make my way to my black 4Runner, hoping I don't run into Captain Sexy himself.

As fate would have it, I am not that lucky. Cursing my luck, I keep my head down and dig into my bag for my keys, feeling his stare across the small back parking lot. I spot Captain Sexy leaning against the trunk of a blue minivan, his legs crossed at the ankles, and his huge tanned arms crossed over his broad chest. I try not to stare but my mouth waters looking at the full sleeve he has inked on his left arm, just begging me to take a lick.

He catches me staring, while I almost walk right into the back corner of my SUV. *Way to be cool, Callie!* I hear him call out to me, "Hey, Cupcake! Be seeing you soon." Then the cocky bastard winks at me and my panties catch fire. I have got to get home before I embarrass myself any further.

The short drive home—curse this town for being so small—did nothing to calm my libido. Even with the A/C on full blast, my skin is still hot all over. *What has that man done to me?* If I'm feeling like this after one brief encounter, I'll never survive an actual date. I can't believe I told him "no" when my lady bits were screaming "hell yeah". I walk in the door and drop my stuff down on the table. I hear Ava in the kitchen and rush in to tell her all about my brush with hotness.

"Everything go OK at the shop today?" Ava's standing in the kitchen, drinking a glass of sweet tea and looking through the mail. My bestie is so pretty with golden blond hair, baby blue eyes, and a runner's body I'd kill for. Why she's still single, I'll never know.

"Sure! If you count running into the three hottest guys on the planet, then yes, everything was great at the shop today."

"Three hottest guys? In this Podunk town? Spill," she says in disbelief.

"Hey, I love this town! You're gonna love it too. Just wait."

"Yeah, we'll see. Now, tell me about these hotties and quit stalling."

"Fine," I tell her with feigned exasperation. "After I dropped cupcakes off to Sophie's Boutique, which you're gonna love BTDubs. Sophie is a real sweetheart and her shop has some amazing stuff.

"Anyway, I then dropped some off at Davis Auto next door. Let me tell you, that is the place where all panties go to melt and ovaries go to combust. No joke, extreme sexiness must be a requirement to work there because those boys scream sex god."

"Well, well, well, little Miss I Don't Have Time to Date. Sure seems like you're interested in dating now, huh?" she says with a smirk.

"I don't have time to date, but I'm not blind. Or dead. There is nothing wrong with examining the merchandise," I say with a small shrug, pretending to be unaffected.

"You know I've known you since kindergarten, right? I can read you like a damn book. You are seriously swooning right now. I can hear your uterus sighing dreamily while your hoo-ha does jazz hands."

I toss a throw pillow at her. "Shut up! If you saw these guys, you'd be acting the same way. You'll see what I mean when you meet them."

"Can't wait," she deadpans. "I need to get my feet wet in this town anyway."

"Oh, is that what you're getting wet? I thought it was something else." Now it's her turn to throw a pillow at me. "What's for dinner anyway? I'm starved."

"Do I look like your personal chef?" she asks me with a cocked brow.

"No, you look like my best friend who loves me and wants to feed me after a long day at the bakery." I give her my best pout with extra sappy puppy dog eyes for good measure.

"Girl, those eyes don't work on me. I invented that

look." Damn it, she's right. No one gives a pout better than Ava. I've seen grown men fall to their knees to please her with just one pout.

"Fine, let's go get a pizza. I'm done working in kitchens for today." I grab my keys, putting my debit card, driver's license, and favorite lip gloss in my pockets, and head for the door.

* * *

Ava and I are jamming out with the windows down when we pull into the cute little pizza place in town, Big Mike's. Starving, we both jump out of my SUV and make our way into the restaurant. It's a small mom and pop place with red checkered tablecloths and big comfy booths. It smells like cheesy garlic heaven and has pictures of family and locals donning the walls.

I come to a complete stop when I open the front door. *Well, fuck sticks! If it isn't Captain Sexy again and his Merry Band of Panty-Melters.* Determined to show him that he has no effect on me—even my vagina coughs a "yeah right" at me—I head straight to the hostess stand.

"Just two?" the tall drink of teenage awkwardness asks me and Ava.

"Just two, please." I throw in a "sweetie", hoping to make him less nervous. Clearly, he's smitten with Ava and can't help but ogle her. Who can blame him? Ava's gorgeous. I'm quietly hoping he'll take us to any table that isn't near Team Hottie, but again that bitch Fate is out to get me.

"Is this table OK?" He takes us to one just a table away from the three most gorgeous men I've ever seen.

"It's fine, honey, thanks," I tell him, secretly wishing he'd move us. He hands us two menus and promises to be right back to take our drink order.

"Who is the table of deliciousness that keeps looking over here?" I pretend not to hear Ava and keep staring at my menu, reading absolutely nothing, just staring at the words.

"Girl, I know you heard me. Are those the guys that had you creaming your panties earlier?"

"Sweet Jesus, would you keep your voice down," I hiss at her. Before I can say anything else, Captain Sexy comes strutting our way. That man has swagger for days. Those thick thighs, corded forearms—every girl loves arm porn—and the most stunning blue eyes I have ever seen. He smells so masculine like broken hearts, bad decisions, a damn good time, and a hint of motor oil.

"Uh, Callie? You got… a little bit of something right there," Ava says, implying I'm drooling, which of course I'm not. Am I? I furiously blush and kick her under the table.

"Aren't you gonna introduce me to your friend, Cupcake?" Asher asks me.

"She's so rude. I'm Ava. And you are?" she pretends

to be demure and gingerly offers him her hand. Of course, I roll my eyes at her theatrics.

"I'm Asher, Cupcake's date later this week. That's my friend, Dane, and my brother, Christian," he says, pointing to the other Hotties.

"Please don't call me 'Cupcake'. And we're not going on a date."

"So your mouth says, but your body says something else." He's totally right, but I'm not giving in just yet.

"You have no idea what my body's saying," I lie. Seductively, he leans into me, his hot mouth just barely brushing the shell of my ear. I feel the warmth of his body so close to mine. My heart pounds in my chest and my breath quickens as he whispers so only I can hear.

"I know exactly what your body's saying, sweetheart. Don't fight it. I can tell you want me just as much as I want you by the way you're holding your breath right now. I can see your pulse at the base of your delicate neck picking up. I can feel the heat radiating off you in waves right now." He gently brushes the back of his knuckles against the bare skin of my arms and I break out in goosebumps. "If I could touch that sweet pussy of yours right now, I bet it'd be wet for me." *Holy fuck balls!!!* "You promised it'd taste as sweet as it looks, right?" He pulls back and smirks, knowing the effect he has on me. *Smug Bastard!*

"I don't know what that man said to you, but judging by your reaction, I think I'm gonna go sit at the other table with Dane and Christian." I glare at Ava, willing her to stay, but that bitch just keeps walking. *Best Friend my ass!*

"Well, Cupcake, now that we're alone…"

"This is still not a date. Just a coincidence that we ran into each other." I try to shake off the lust coursing through my body.

"Eh, I think it's fate. Give it up, Cupcake, you're gonna be mine sooner or later." He says, leaning back in his chair, all man spread and gorgeous.

"Why? Because every other girl throws her panties at you, the second they get a glimpse of those dimples and all that sexiness?"

"Aw, babe, you think I'm sexy?" *Damn it, Callie!* "I think you're sexy too. And the way you blush makes me think you don't even know just how sexy you are." I can feel my cheeks getting hot again. "See what I mean."

"Alright, look. I'm starving and it's been a long day. I'm too tired to fight your pitiful attempt at hitting on me. The least you can do is feed me while my defenses are down." I lift my chin in defiance, a poor effort at acting like I'm not gonna give into this man in the very near future. But he doesn't know that.

"Pitiful attempt? Keep telling yourself that, Cupcake. You know you're gonna be mine sooner or later, but I'll let you run for now. Anything worthwhile is worth the chase."

Made in the USA
Middletown, DE
29 April 2021